LONE WOLF and CUB

by
KAZUO KOIKE
and
GOSEKI KOJIMA

cover by
BILL SIENKIEWICZ

第13巻

小島剛夕　小池一夫

Kazuo Koike STORY	Goseki Kojima ART

Bill Sienkiewicz
COVER ILLUSTRATION

David Lewis, Alex Wald
ENGLISH ADAPTATION

Willie Schubert LETTERING	Paul Guinan PRODUCTION
Rick Oliver EDITOR	Rick Obadiah PUBLISHER
Alex Wald ART DIRECTOR	Kathy Kotsivas OPERATIONS DIRECTOR
Mike McCormick PRODUCTION MANAGER	Kurt Goldzung SALES DIRECTOR

Lone Wolf and Cub (Kozure Okami) © 1988 Kazuo Koike and Goseki Kojima.

English translation © 1988 First Comics, Inc. and Global Communications Corporation.

Cover illustration © 1988 Bill Sienkiewicz.

Published monthly in the United States of America by First Comics, Inc., 435 N. LaSalle, Chicago Il 60610, and Studio Ship, Inc. under exclusive license by Global Communications Corporation, Musashiya Building, 4th Floor, 27-10, Aobadai 1-Chome, Meguro-Ku, Tokyo, 153 Japan, owner of world wide publishing rights to the property Lone Wolf and Cub.

Lone Wolf and Cub #13 (ISBN 0-915419-33-5) © 1988 First Comics, Inc. and Global Communications Corporation. All rights reserved.

First printing, May 1988.

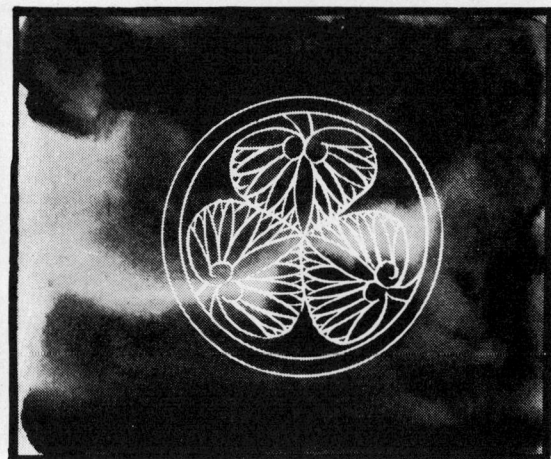

ITTO OGAMI!

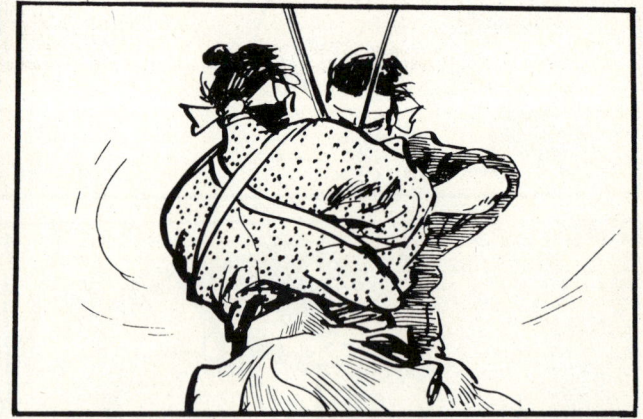

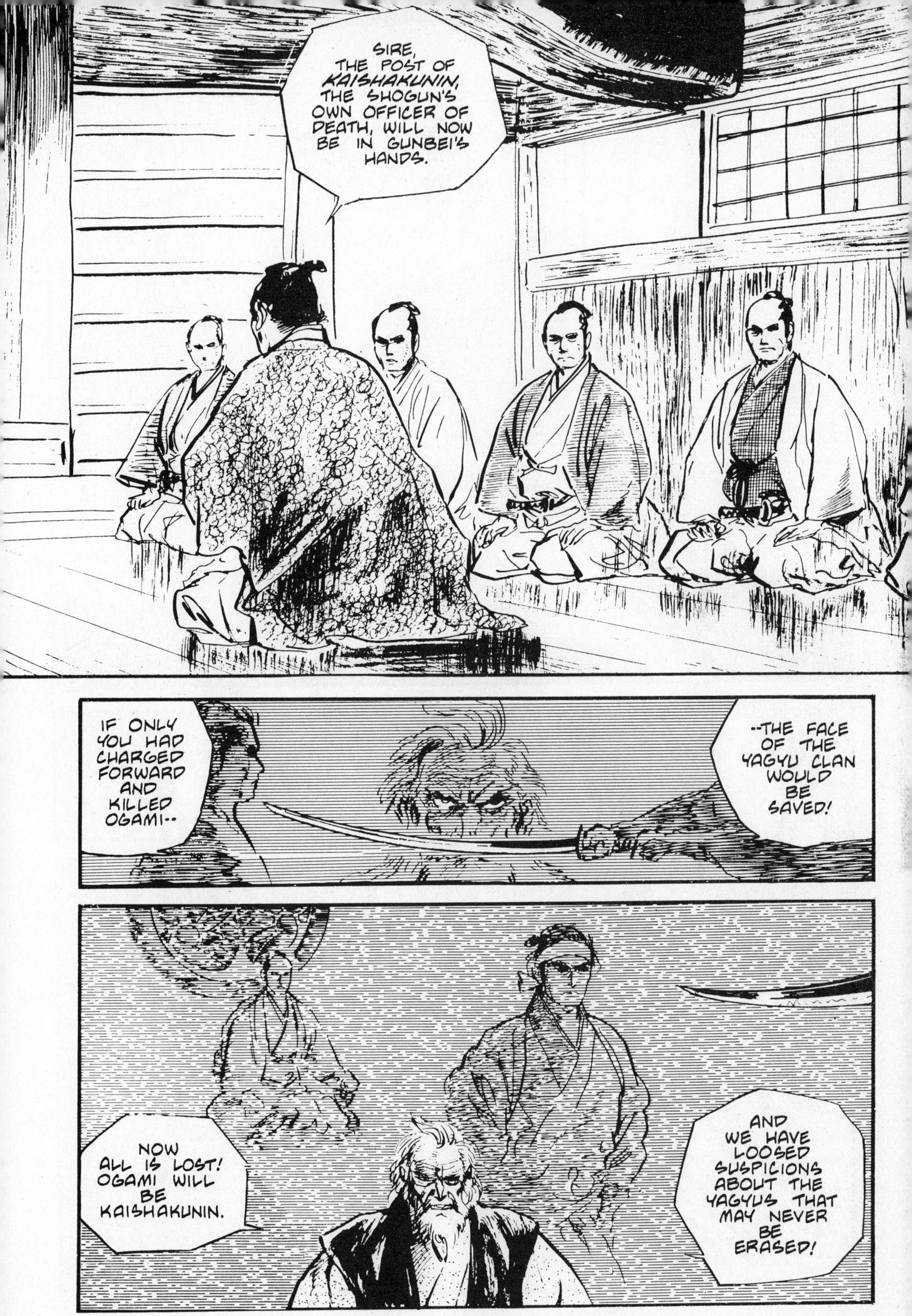

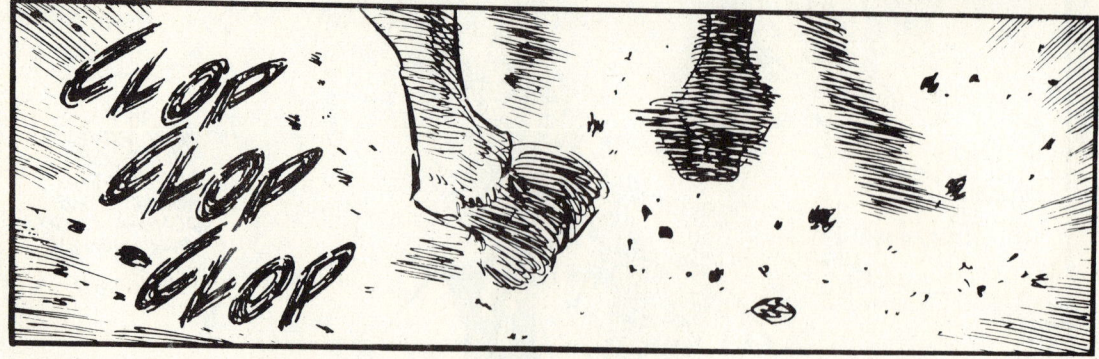

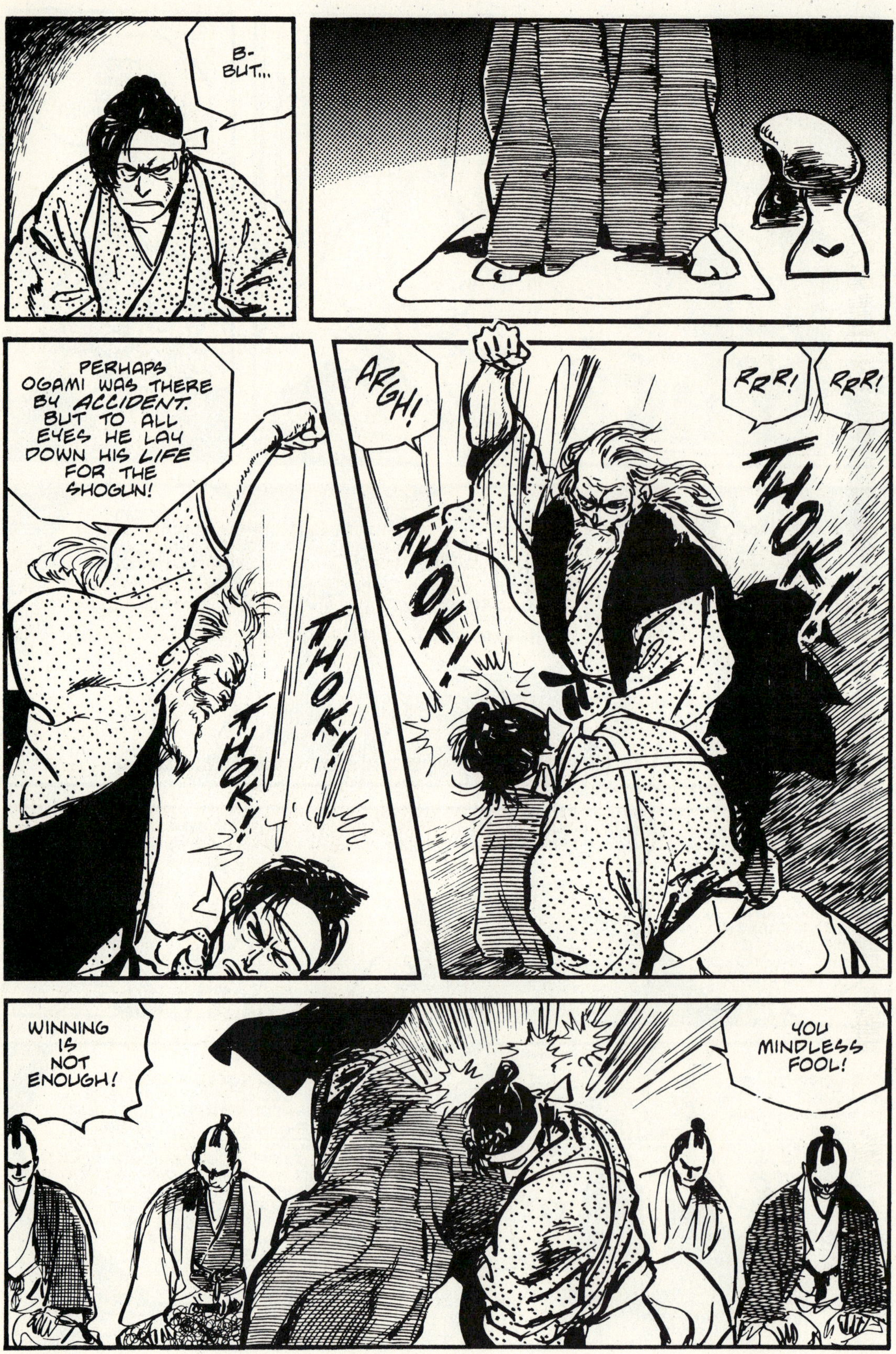

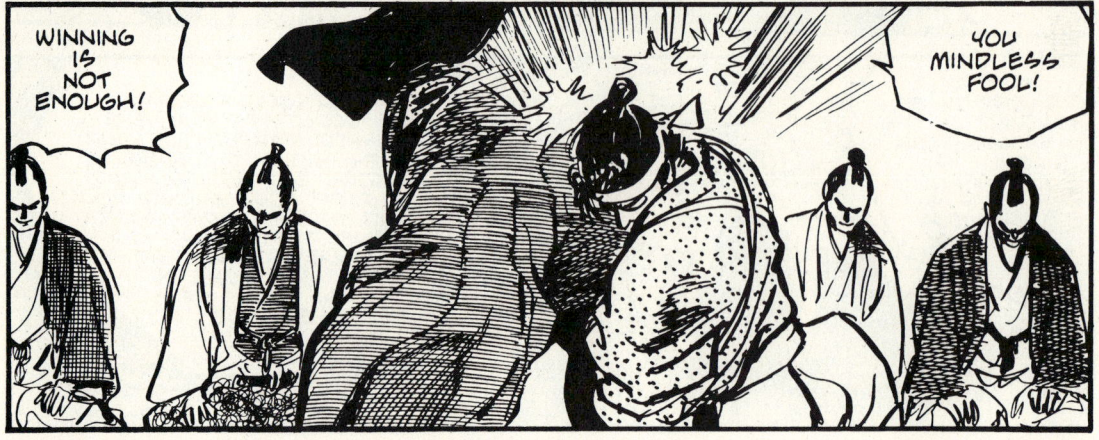

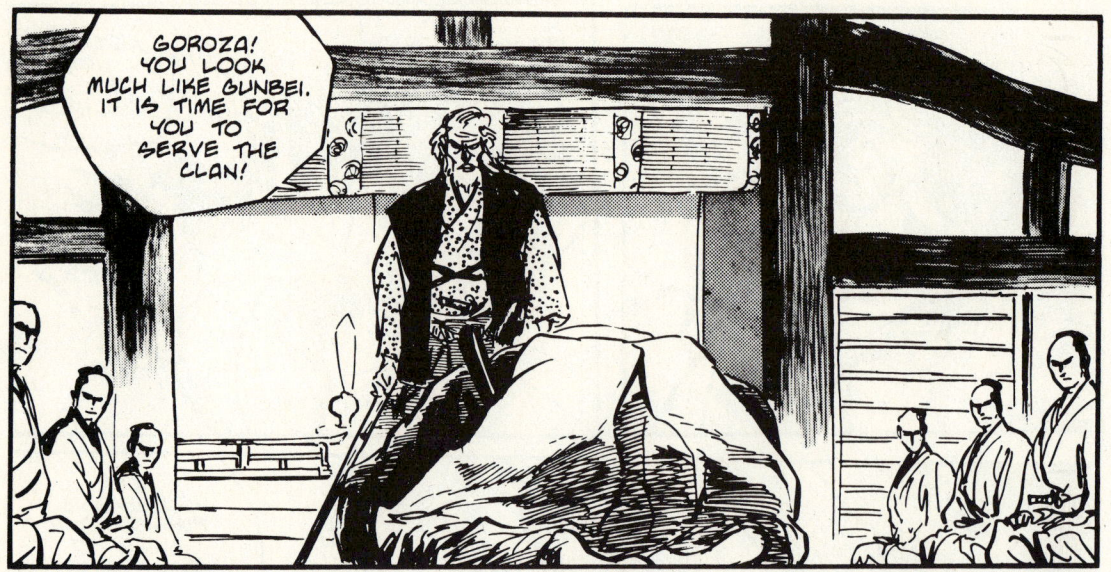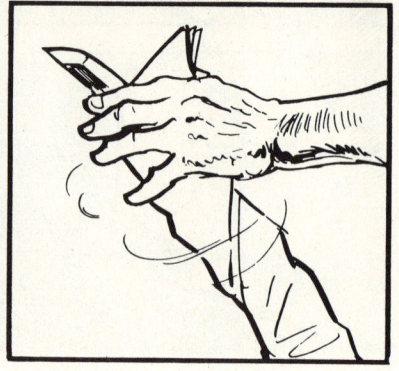

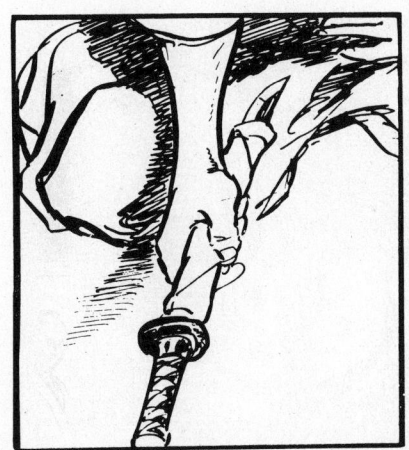

BE IT ONLY IN *NAME*, THE SWORD OF THE *YAGYU* HAS BEEN *BESTED* BY ITTO OGAMI! FROM NOW ON THE *OGAMI* FAMILY WILL WEAR THE HOLLYHOCK CREST OF THE SHOGUN. *KAISHAKUNIN*, THE OFFICER OF DEATH!

THE DAIMYO OF SIXTY PROVINCES WILL DREAD *HIM*. *HIS* FAMILY WILL GROW IN POWER. *HIS* SWORD WILL GROW IN FAME!

WE NAME YOU *KAISHAKUNIN* TO OUR LORD THE SHOGUN. PERFORM YOUR DUTIES WELL.

THE HONOR IS TOO GREAT FOR MY HUMBLE SELF. I RECEIVE IT IN ALL HUMILITY.

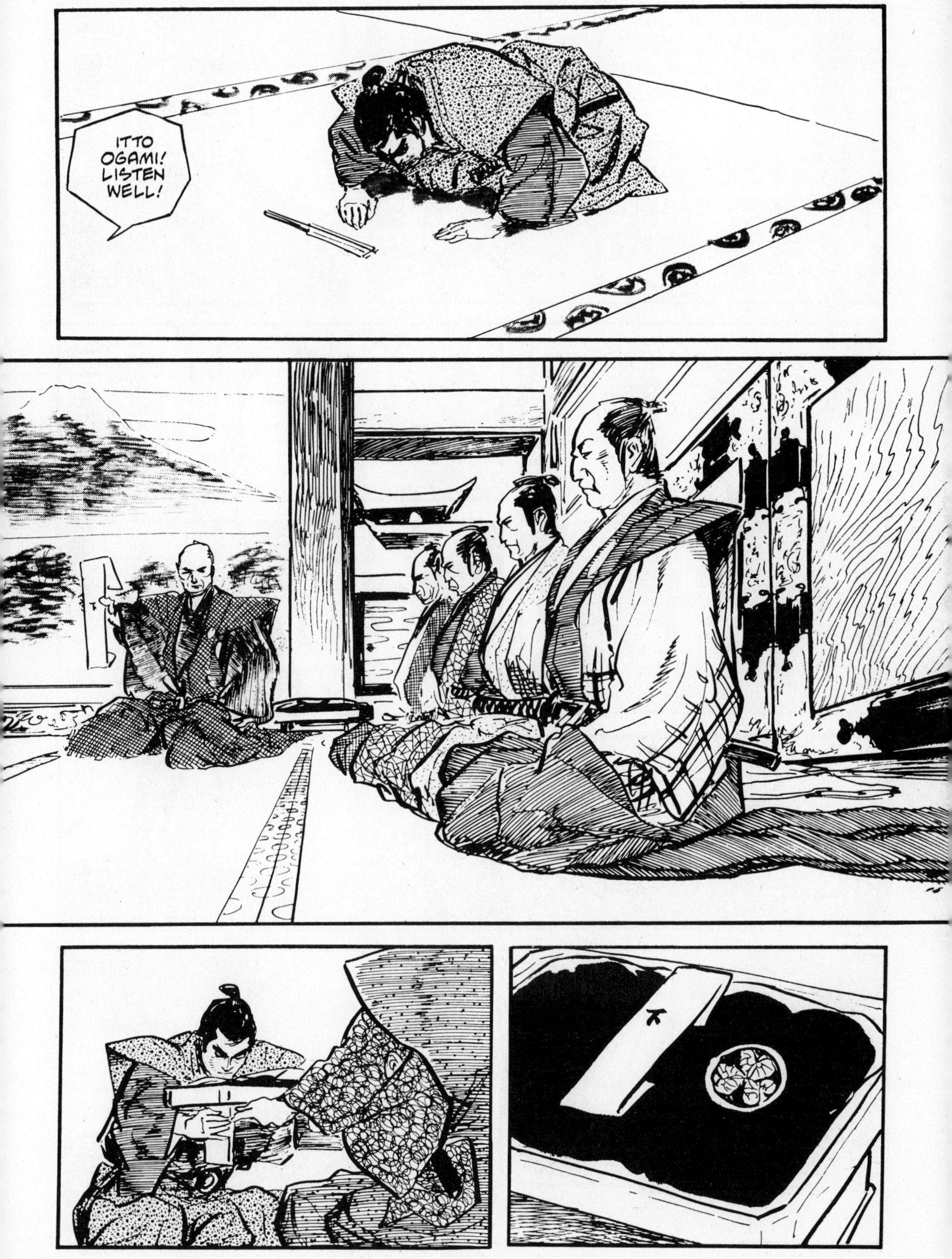

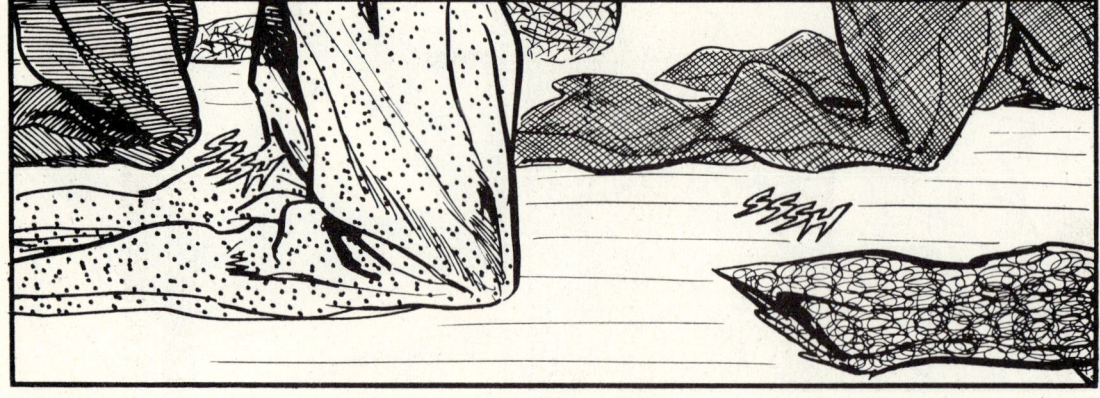

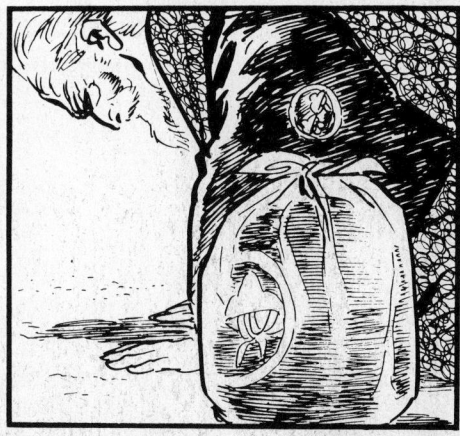

LORD RETSUDO, WHAT IS THIS URGENT BUSINESS YOU CLAIM?

TRULY AN ACT WORTHY OF THE YAGYU.

IT IS MY SHAME TO REPORT THAT, AT FIRST, WE ELDERS FAILED TO NOTICE THAT GUNBEI'S SWORD HAD POINTED TOWARD OUR LORD, OR THAT OGAMI HAD INTERPOSED HIS BODY TO BLOCK IT. GUNBEI'S VICTORY SEEMED CLEAR TO ALL. WE WERE PREPARED TO DECIDE THE APPOINTMENT WITHOUT AWAITING AN OFFICIAL JUDGMENT.

IT WAS AT THE INSISTENCE OF LORD SHUBO MATSUDAIRA, WITH HIS KEEN PERCEPTION--

THAT WE CRAVED OUR LORD'S OWN JUDGMENT. HE GRACIOUSLY OBSERVED THAT IT WAS INDEED AS SHUBO SAID.

YET I AM TRULY IMPRESSED, LORD YAGYU. GUNBEI'S DEATH WAS MAGNIFICENT.

A SIGN OF SUPERB RESOLUTION. THIS IN ITSELF SAVES OUR OWN FACE FOR HAVING INITIALLY SELECTED HIM KAISHAKUNIN.

LORD SHUBO SPOKE TRULY.

BUT IT WOULD SEEM HE SPOKE PERHAPS TOO HASTILY.

"There is no retracting this regrettable incident. Yet those who serve the Shogun are always prepared to seek life in death. Gunbei was no exception. Moreover, it was a contest he had won..."

"If he had turned his sword toward our lord only because Ogami was standing there... there might have been a different decision..."

"Truly."

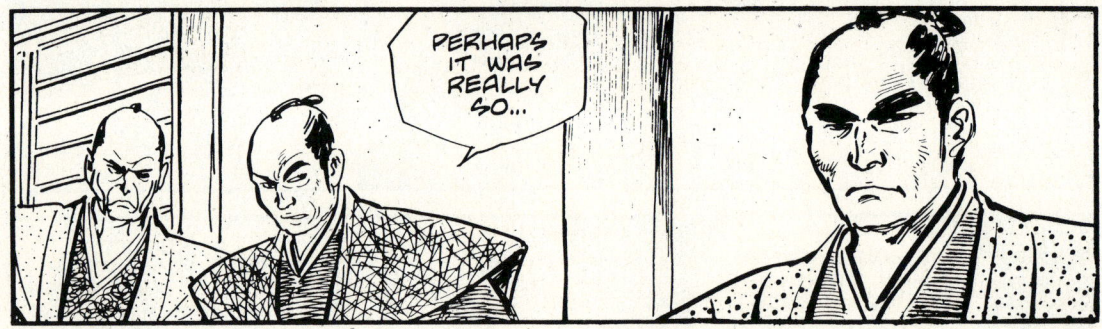

"Perhaps it was really so..."

"Now that Lord Ogami has been chosen kaishakunin, the Yagyu clan puts behind all past unpleasantness. We will support him without regret."

"I thank you for your gracious words."

*KAGEMUSHA-- "SHADOW WARRIOR." A SAMURAI ASSIGNED TO IMPERSONATE A HIGHER RANKING NOBLE.

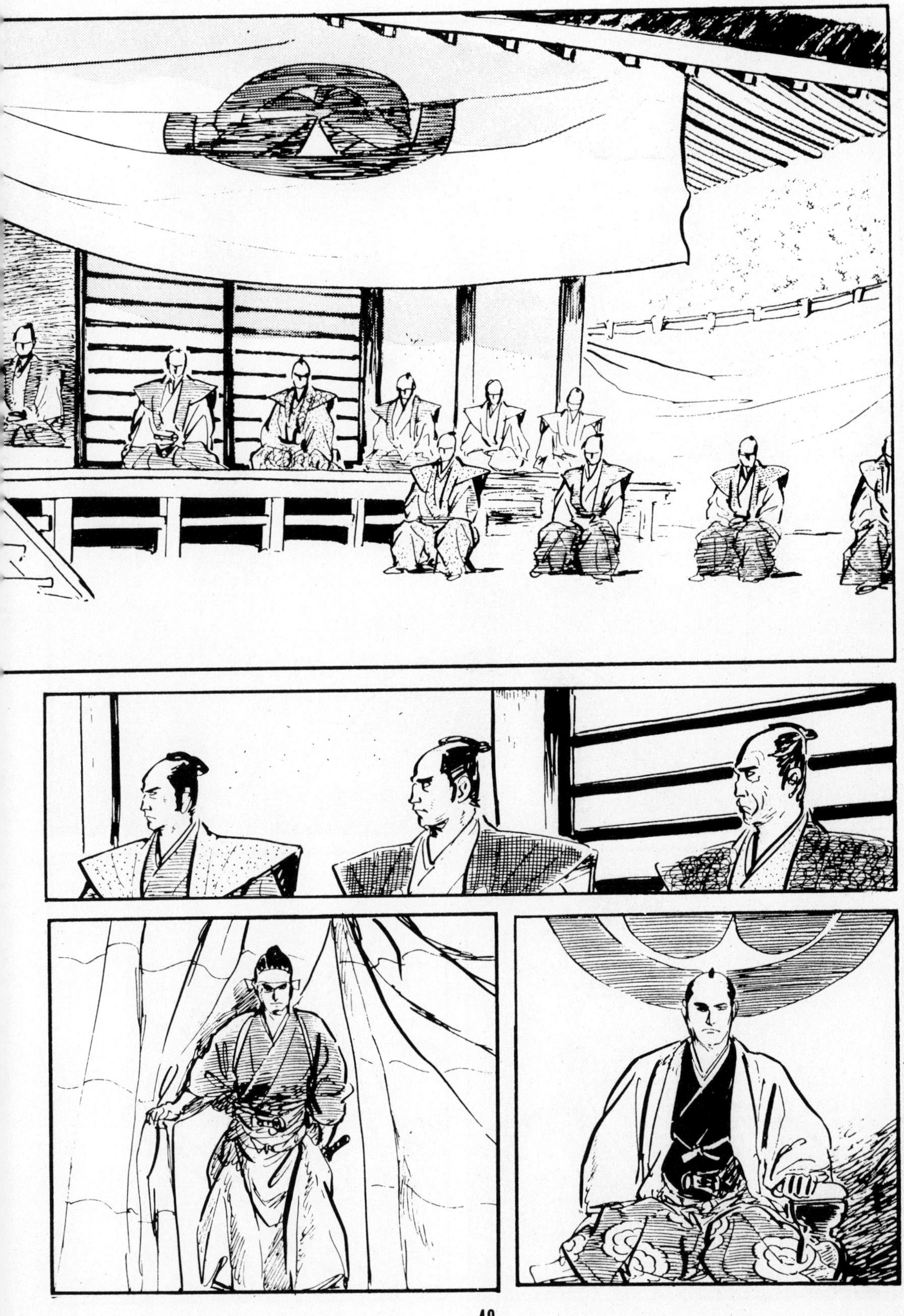

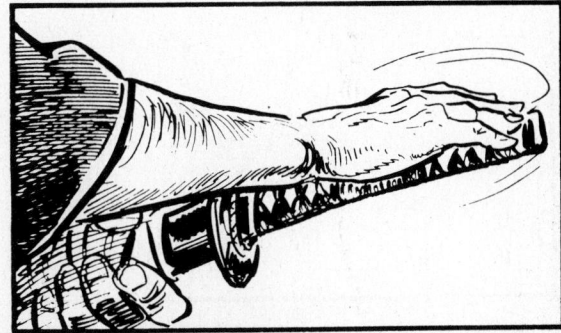

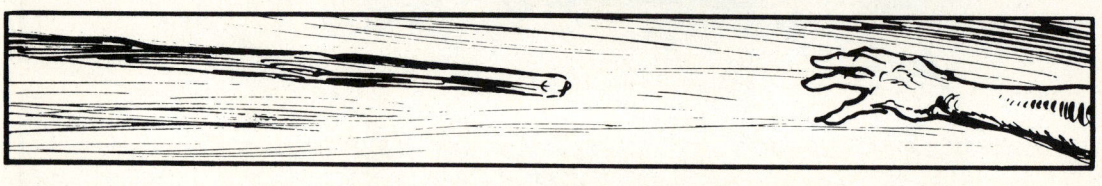
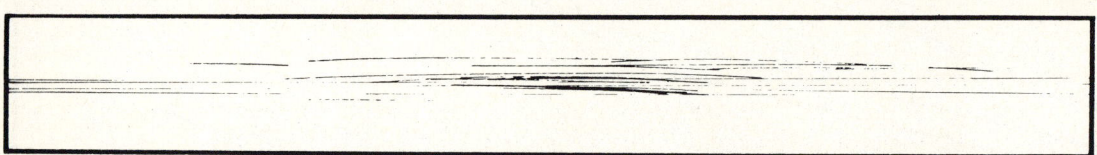

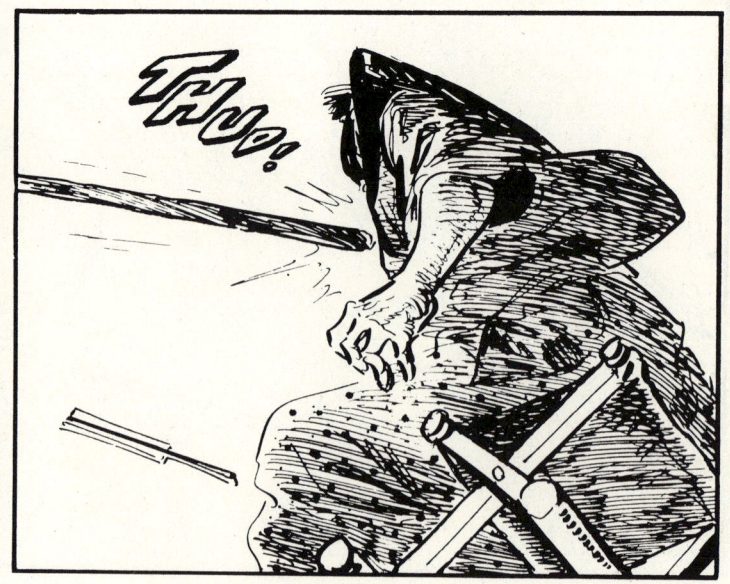

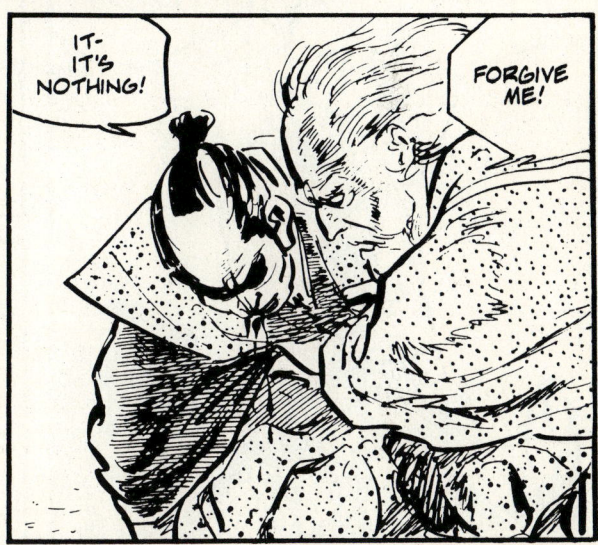

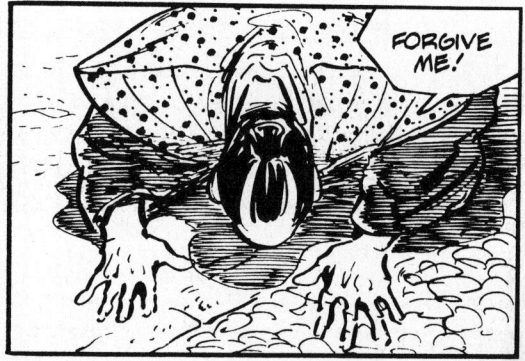

WHY WAS YAGYU SO HUNGRY TO HAVE THE KAISHAKUNIN FOR HIS OWN?

ONLY WHEN I FIND THE ANSWER CAN WE LEAVE THESE ENDLESS SIX ROADS. ONLY THEN DO WE BEGIN OUR JOURNEY TO REVENGE.

LORD SHUBO...

BIOGRAPHY

KAZUO KOIKE

Kazuo Koike is considered to be one of Japan's most successful writers and a master scriptwriter for the graphic story genre. He is perhaps best known in the U.S. for his screenplay for the feature film "Shogun Assassin," a re-edited version of the Japanese film "Kozure Okami," based on the **Lone Wolf and Cub** stories. Mr. Koike currently operates a publishing/production company for comics, Studio Ship, Inc., which publishes the works of Japan's major comics writers and artists in both book and magazine format. Mr. Koike is also the founder of Gekiga-Sonjuko, a school which offers a two year course for aspiring professional artists and writers.

GOSEKI KOJIMA

Goseki Kojima made his debut as a comic artist in 1967 with "Oboro-Junin-Cho." With his unique style Mr. Kojima created a new form of expressive visual interpretation for the graphic storytelling medium, and established for himself a position as a master craftsman with his groundbreaking work on **Lone Wolf and Cub**. Other works by Mr. Kojima in collaboration with Mr. Koike are "Kawaite Soro," "Kubikiri Asa," "Hanzo-No-Mon," "Tatamidori Kasajiro," "Do-Chi-Shi," and "Bohachi Bushido."

小池一夫　小島剛夕

NEXT MONTH

A simple gesture of atonement for the death of a serving girl, an innocent accidently sacrificed to the way of the assassin, leads the Lone Wolf to risk his freedom and his life when he discovers the meaning of the "Black Wind."